GOALS TO GOLD

TRACK & FIELD STORIES FOR YOUNG READERS

JARED DEES

For more information, visit jareddees.com.

Paperback: ISBN 978-1-954135-14-7
eBook: ISBN 978-1-954135-15-4

For Coach Bill "Doc" Scott

CONTENTS

INTRODUCTION

Track & field may seem simple. We run; we jump; or we throw. But the many events that make up track & field as well as cross country can unlock incredible opportunities in your life. They can open your mind to the possibilities you never thought your body could achieve. Run faster. Jump higher. Throw farther. Set goals, work hard to reach them, and find both external and internal rewards.

In this book you will find stories of some of the greatest track & field athletes of all time. As you read these tales, you will discover some common elements of their journeys. Each of their lives and backgrounds are unique. Some athletes came from difficult childhoods, while others grew up with the advantage of a supportive family. Regardless of their personal life stories, the same themes appear again and again. These themes can guide you along your track & field journey.

How do you get faster? How do you get stronger? How do you build up the mental toughness necessary to succeed in track & field? You will need to find some help in the gap between your goals today and the gold medals you could earn in the future.

According to the stories in this book, here is what you will need to seek and find in order to reach your highest potential:

FIND A ROLE MODEL FOR INSPIRATION.

Watch the Olympic Games. Attend professional races. Watch videos of winning performances in your event. Find someone you can look up to and aspire to be like some day. So many of the men and women in this book were inspired by the successful athletes of the generation before them.

For instance, a young sprinter named Jackie Joyner-Kersee saw Evelyn Ashford compete at the Olympics on TV and realized she could compete on a world stage too some day. Sydney McLaughlin-Levrone looked up to sprinter Allyson Felix as a kid, then found herself running on the same relay team with Felix years later. Paula Radcliffe attended her first London Marathon, saw Ingrid Kristiansen's win, and told her dad "I'd love to do that." Decades later, she set a world record in that very race.

We need people to look up to. Someone out there is showing you the work ethic needed to succeed. Follow in their footsteps, then compete and forge your own path. Become an inspiration for others who will come after you.

FIND A GOOD COACH (OR THEY WILL FIND YOU).

The men and women in this book did not achieve success through sheer talent and hard work. They all had the support of coaches who saw their potential and pushed them to the limits of their abilities. You will find P.E. teachers who saw greatness in middle school students. You will find professional coaches whose training methods enabled new levels of success. There are spouses, siblings, and parents who have all helped coach these men and women to success—at both a young age and well into professional careers.

Find a good coach at your school, in your home, or in a local organization. As you progress, you will discover new coaches and new men and women to push you to the next level. Listen to them. Work hard for them. Thank them for the time and dedication they put into your success.

FIND TEAMMATES THAT PUSH YOU TO YOUR HIGHEST POTENTIAL.

There are so many examples of teammates and training partners pushing the men and women in this book towards success. Roger Bannister could not have broken the 4-minute mile barrier without two Olympic athletes pacing him around the track. It is no coincidence (or maybe it is an incredible coincidence) that Wilma Rudolph's TSU college teammates were the same women running with her in the Olympics. It is tempting to see track & field as an individual sport, but the reality is that no one competes at the highest level alone.

FIND RIVALRIES TO PUSH YOU BEYOND YOUR HIGHEST EXPECTATIONS.

You will come across some of the greatest rivalries in all of sports within these pages. Put simply, to win in track & field is to run faster, throw further, or jump higher than someone else. When you have someone to beat, you often push yourself beyond what you think you can accomplish. The rivalries in this book (whether friendly or hostile) are incredible. They include:

- Carl Lewis vs. Mike Powell
- Usain Bolt vs. Tyson Gay
- Sydney McLaughlin-Levrone vs. Dalilah Muhammad
- Germany vs. United States

Competition from the athletes on your team or competing teams should push you to train harder in practice. These rivals should be so difficult to beat that you must push yourself beyond your limits in a meet.

FIND THE RIGHT EVENT.

Many of the athletes in this book had to prove to themselves and others that they could compete in new events. It is easy to get stuck in a certain identity with a certain event. As you grow, however, you may find your body and mind are better suited for something else. That slight change and experimentation may lead to unbelievable success in more events than you thought possible.

When Paula Radcliffe focused on training for marathons, she had a breakthrough in shorter-distance events as well. Usain Bolt's coaches thought he should be a 400-meter runner, but Bolt proved his greatest potential in the shorter distances. Carl Lewis grew up as a long jumper, but his training spilled over into the sprinting events as well. Jackie Joyner-Kersee was a long jumper too, but she had so much athletic ability that she focused on the many events in the heptathlon to achieve greatness. The same went for all-around athlete Jim Thorpe, who won both the pentathlon and the decathlon in his Olympic competition.

Broaden your focus. Try new events. See how you progress in your main event by training for other events instead. These slight or massive shifts in focus can open up new potential you didn't know you had.

FIND YOUR FORM.

All coaches teach ideal running form and ideal field event techniques. Everyone must learn the tried-and-true techniques when they start out in an event. At the same time, no one is built in the same way. We are each born with different body types and develop in different ways. Therefore, no two people will have exactly the same running style or field event technique. They key is to make improvements upon what you do now, constantly getting better.

Many of the athletes in this book learned the ideal techniques, but succeeded as they developed their own style and form. Michael Johnson's upright style was supposed to slow him down, but he became the fastest man in the world in his events. It was painful to watch Emil Zátopek run long distances with his tortured style and heaving breaths, but still he won. Ryan Crouser uses his academic ability to experiment and study slight tweaks to his approach in shot put. Dick Fosbury's experiments in the high jump in high school and college not only led to an Olympic gold medal, they completely changed the way high jumpers after him leaped over the bar. Almost everyone soon adopted his unique form.

You can't win without elite control of your body. You can't ignore the fundamentals of form and technique. You can and should, however, experiment and make slight tweaks to compete at your highest level. Find your strengths and capitalize on them. Listen to your coaches, and work with them to try new things to find what works best for you.

FIND GOALS BEYOND ANYONE'S EXPECTATIONS (INCLUDING YOUR OWN).

Make sure your goals aren't too small. You do not know the fullness of your potential. You will surprise yourself constantly in your athletic career. Therefore, set big goals. Set goals with better times and distances than you think are possible.

So many of the men and women in this book were chasing world records as they began their professional careers. Time and time again, however, they surprised even themselves as they broke through barriers that no one on earth had broken before. Go back and watch the races. Watch their reactions to their times, heights, and distances. Shock and joy can be seen again and again. They did not know their own abilities.

Roger Bannister didn't just set out to win, he set a goal to become the first man to break the 4-minute-mile barrier. Once he showed it was possible, dozens and then thousands followed in his wake. This is a common theme among many of the record-breaking performances in this book. What was once thought impossible suddenly became possible, and then many more people followed suit, chasing a new standard to beat.

Ironically, failing to reach your goals can be just as motivating as passing them. The Olympics occur every four years. A failure in the trials one year motivated so many athletes in this book to return to training with such determination that they made the next attempt at completely heightened levels of competitiveness. Failure is never final. Betty Robinson was nearly paralyzed in a plane crash as she prepared for a return to the Olympics. Walking barely seemed like a possibility at the time, but eventually she found the drive to make her miraculous return. The setbacks may seem like the end now, but they can be the fuel you need to succeed beyond anything you thought possible.

Set big goals. Set bigger goals than you even think are possible today. Welcome failure as feedback and adjust your training to break through the mental barriers of what you or others think is possible. You do not know how fast you can run, how far you can throw, or how high or far you can jump.

Don't believe me? Turn the page and follow along with some of the greatest track & field athletes of all time. They met adversity, found a lot of help along the way, and overcame the greatest of challenges.

May you find inspiration in their successes and failures as you begin your track & field career.

Ready? Set. Go!

COROEBUS OF ELIS
RUN YOUR RACE

In 776 BC, Coroebus, a cook and a baker from the Greek city-state of Elis, stood with his hands outstretched at the starting line of the first recorded Olympics. It was the one event of the day and the only event in the entire Olympics at the time. He was running against 19 other athletes in an event called the *stade*.

The *stade*, from which we get the English word *stadium*, was a race 600 Ancient Greek feet in length, which is an estimated 150-200 meters. The track in Olympia did not resemble the oval layout we have today. There was only one long, straight track for runners to compete on.

The games were more than a fun competition; they were a religious duty. According to legend, the Olympics were established by Hercules, the son of the Greek god Zeus. Competitors and spectators came from all over Ancient Greece to compete in memory of Hercules and to honor Zeus. The competition took place near a temple dedicated to Zeus and the track was believed to have been created by Hercules himself to honor his father. Hercules took 200 paces in a straight line to establish the distance for the race.

The 776 BC race was not the first Olympic stade, but marked the first time that a champion would be named and immortalized by Ancient Greek historians in their record books. Each man in the race aimed to prove he was the fastest man in the world. But none of them were professional athletes like we have today. Like Coroebus, they were ordinary men with ordinary jobs. Yet Coroebus was about to become world famous.

Coroebus was joined at the starting line by representatives from many city-states throughout Ancient Greece. During this and all subsequent Olympic Games, a required peace pact was put in place for each participating kingdom. No city-state could be at war with another during the games. The sole competition in the Ancient Greek world would take place on the singular track in a singular event.

There was no gun to begin the race. Instead a loud horn was blown at the starting line. Stones would be used as starting blocks many years later in the games, but for now all competitors stood upright with hands out in front of them. It is often noted that the athletes in the Ancient Olympics competed in the nude, but that tradition did not begin for another fifty years after Coroebus's race.

The thousands of people in the crowd lined along the hills on each side of the stade stood in silence. Then the horn resounded through the hills. The men took off, vying for position. Their feet pounded on the flattened ground of clay with a thin layer of sand on top that was added for traction. Cheers came from both sides of the track as one man emerged in front.

Coroebus flew past the judges as the undisputed winner of the Olympics! Cheers erupted from the crowds, especially from those attending from his home city of Elis. Coroebus turned to congratulate his competition before standing alone before the crowd.

His prize was on the way. A representative of the games was bringing a crown of olive branches made from a tree growing next to the temple of Zeus. The branches had been cut with a pair of golden scissors and placed upon a table in the temple of Hera, the wife of Zeus, until a winner had been determined. From there, the judges retrieved the crown to deliver it to the victor and place it upon his head. There was no gold, silver, or bronze medal. There was no prize for second or third place. The sacred prize from the gods was awarded to only one winner. Coroebus of Elis was crowned the first Olympian and would maintain his title as the fastest man in the world for the next four years, until the next Olympic stade would take place.

As the years went on, more events were included in the Olympics. First, additional running events were added to the Olympics. Then jumping and throwing events took place as well. Soon after that wrestling, boxing, and horse-racing events became a part of the games. These competitions and the peacetime that came with them occurred every four years for more than 1,000 years. When the Roman Empire took control of Ancient Greece, the importance of the games diminished. It is unknown when exactly the last ancient Olympics took place, but it was likely sometime in either the fourth or fifth centuries. The modern Olympic Games were revived in Athens, Greece in 1896, and competitors return again every four years to see who is the best at various events.

REFLECTION QUESTIONS

In your experience, what are some of the similarities and differences between the 776 BC Olympics and the Olympics today?

What do you think life was like for Coroebus after the Olympics?

What has been your greatest accomplishment so far as an athlete?

JIM THORPE

PERSEVERE THROUGH ADVERSITY

Although he was baptized James Francis Thorpe in 1887, Jim Thorpe's given name was *Wa-Tho-Huk*. He was born into the Sac and Fox tribe in Indian Territory, which would eventually become the state of Oklahoma. His native name means "Bright Path," but his legendary rise to athletic greatness was anything but bright. Thorpe overcame tremendous adversity and opposition in his athletic journey.

Thorpe was often angry and despondent as a youth. He lost his twin brother to pneumonia at the age of nine. His mother died in childbirth when he was 11, sending him into a spiral of depression. After his mother died, Thorpe left his father's house to run away to work on a horse ranch.

He returned home at 16, but decided with his father to move to Pennsylvania to attend Carlisle Indian Industrial School. Thorpe dropped out of school, however, when his father died after a hunting accident, and returned to work as a horse rancher.

He might have stayed in Oklahoma as a farm hand for the rest of his life, but something at school sparked his interest. Before he left, he participated in a few track meets for Carlisle. He also convinced his track coach that he could play football for the Indians. That coach was the legendary football icon "Pop" Warner.

Coach Warner thought Thorpe should stick with track. The young man weighed only 155 pounds at the time. Still, Thorpe convinced his coach to let him run the ball at football practice. The first time he held the ball, he was so fast that the defenders could barely touch him. The team now had a star running back. Thorpe went on to earn third-team All-American before leaving school that year.

When Jim Thorpe returned to school in 1911, he continued to show coach Warner that he could succeed on the football field. Thorpe led the Carlisle football team to an 11–1 record and was named as a first-team All-American. The Indians would go on to win a national championship the following year in 1912 with an upset victory over Army thanks to team captain Thorpe's outstanding performance.

Prior to that 1912 football season, however, Jim Thorpe found international fame in track & field. He earned a spot on the USA Olympic team in the pentathlon and decathlon. It was the perfect role for him. Thorpe was so versatile, excelling in many sports and events. At Carlisle earlier that year, he had often been the sole participant in many track meets, running multiple events for the school!

In the 1912 Olympics, Jim Thorpe earned gold in the pentathlon, placing first in four of the five events (1st in long jump, 200m, discus, and 1500m, with a 3rd in the javelin throw). He then went on to win gold in the decathlon as well with its 10 events: 100m, long jump, shot put, high jump, 400m, discus, 110m hurdles, pole vault, javelin throw, and 1500m. He placed in the top four of all 10 events, winning first place in the shot put, high jump, 110m hurdles, and 1500m.

But even this great victory couldn't be celebrated without adversity. Leading up to the decathlon, someone had stolen his track shoes. He scrounged around until he could find two mismatched cleats of different sizes, one of which he found in a trash can. He had to wear an extra pair of socks to fit into one of the shoes. The thievery didn't stop him from winning his second gold medal of the games.

Jim Thorpe came home a national hero, with people shouting his name at the welcome home parade. His national championship in football only multiplied his fame. Then in January 1913, reporters investigating his life uncovered evidence that he was paid to play baseball in 1909 and 1910 while he was away from school. This would technically make him a professional athlete, which was a problem. Pros were unable to participate in the Olympics at the time.

Sadly, the Olympics committee disqualified his victories and took away his gold medals. It was sorrowful news for Thorpe, who didn't realize he was making a mistake at the time. Many believe the decision to strip Thorpe of the medals was motivated by racial discrimination. Thorpe was a Native American. Many Native Americans were not granted U.S. citizenship until 1924. Therefore, the reports may have been an effort to attack Jim Thorpe's character.

Fortunately, the national controversy sparked interest in Thorpe from professional baseball teams. He had multiple offers, and he officially began his professional baseball career in 1913. That same year he played professional football, and he continued to play both sports for many years. He finally retired from football at the age of 41 in 1928. He was later named the first commissioner of the NFL.

In 1983, almost 30 years after Thorpe's death in 1953, the International Olympic Committee reinstated Jim Thorpe's gold medals. It was proven that the decision to strip Thorpe of the medals was made in error, because evidence was not submitted within 30 days of the win. The reporters dug up the stories about Thorpe's baseball payments nearly six months after the Olympics. Years later in 2022, the IOC also officially named Thorpe as the sole historical winner in the pentathlon and decathlon. He would now rightfully remain an Olympic winner and gold medalist forever.

REFLECTION QUESTIONS

What were some of the greatest challenges for Jim Thorpe to overcome?

What other sports do you (or could you) succeed in beyond track & field?

When have you experienced adversity or challenges in athletics? Did you respond like Jim Thorpe? Why or why not?

JESSE OWENS

TRAIN FOR THE FUTURE

Jesse Owens is possibly the most famous and successful track & field athlete of all time. He won four gold medals in the 1936 Olympic Games for the 100m, 200m, long jump, and 4x100m relay events. A year earlier on May 25, 1935 Owens set four world records within 45 minutes, competing in the 100-yard dash, 220-yard dash, 220-yard hurdles, and long jump. Years later, USA Track & Field would officially name their highest accolade in his name as the Jesse Owens Award. His accomplishments on a worldwide stage were legendary.

As the youngest child of an African American family of 10 children in southern Alabama, his future success was not obvious. His family lived in poor conditions working on a farm. So the Owens family moved to Cleveland, Ohio to find work when Jesse was only nine. Jesse's Southern accent was so thick that his teacher misheard him pronounce his name. She thought he said "Jesse" when he was really saying his nickname "J.C." (for his birth name James Cleveland). But the name "Jesse" stuck with him.

To help his family earn money, Owens had to work after school delivering groceries and other jobs like loading freight cars. Meanwhile, his middle school gym teacher, Charles Riley, saw something in young Owens. Riley encouraged him to join his track team as a sprinter. Since Owens had to work after school, Coach Riley trained the young boy in the hours before school.

At first, Jesse wasn't the fastest kid in the area. He often slowed down if another runner was beating him in a race. Coach Riley pushed the boy to work harder. The coach believed in him more than he believed in himself. Owens would later refer to the man as a second father. And Coach Riley treated him like a second son. In addition to the extra time with him in the mornings, Riley often brought Owens home for meals with his own family. The fact that Riley was white and Owens was black in the 1920s didn't stand in the way of their close relationship.

Coach Riley trained Owens to improve his body, but he also developed the boy's mental toughness. He told Owens to imagine the track was on fire when he ran so that his legs would barely touch the ground. When Owens finished a race with a tense jaw and grimace, Riley took him to the horse racing track and told him to watch the horses and imitate their relaxed form.

Always, Riley taught his signature motto: "Train for four years from next Friday." In other words, focus on long-term goals. Work hard now so that you can find success many years from now. It's not about seeing immediate results.

Owens took these lessons to heart. By his eighth-grade year in 1928, he set junior high records for the high jump and the long jump. He continued to train harder, and in 1930 he set high school records in the long jump, 100-yard dash, and 200-yard dash. He joined the Ohio State University track & field team on a scholarship in 1933, set multiple word records in 1935, and won his four gold medals in the 1936 Olympics.

Four years before winning the gold medals, he was a senior in high school. Four years before that he was in 8th grade, running for a Cleveland gym teacher and coach who believed in him and went out of his way to train him. "Train for four years from next Friday," Coach Riley used to say. Jesse Owens did exactly that and made history.

REFLECTION QUESTIONS

What was some of Coach Riley's best advice for Jesse Owens?

Who are the coaches and mentors that believe in you the most?

Who has helped you and encouraged you in your life? How have they helped?

ELIZABETH "BETTY" ROBINSON

RUN WITH A SMILE

Elizabeth "Betty" Robinson was a young phenom. As a 16-year-old girl from Chicago, she made history in the 1928 Olympic Games by winning gold in the first women's Olympic 100m dash. She remains the youngest woman to win a gold medal in the Olympics. Even more remarkable, the 100m dash in the Olympics was only the third official track meet of her life.

Earlier that year, Robinson's science teacher, Charles Price, saw the girl running to catch a train after school. Price was the coach of the boys track team at Thornton Township High School. There was no girls team at the time. He asked Robinson if she would be willing to run in some indoor track meets that spring. During the Chicago winter, Coach Price had Robinson train by running through the halls of their school.

In her first official indoor track meet, she finished in second place in the 60m. She was just one spot behind Helen Filkey, the reigning female US record holder in the 100m. Two months later she beat Filkey in the 100m and tied the world record in the race. Two months after that she shocked the world by winning the first women's Olympic 100m dash just a few weeks shy of her seventeenth birthday.

The future looked bright for the young, enthusiastic Betty Robinson. She enrolled in Northwestern University to study physical education. Her plan was to return to the Olympics in 1932 to defend her title and win another gold medal. Then she could become the coach of the next women's Olympic team, in 1936.

But in 1931 a tragedy took place. Robinson joined her cousin for a short airplane ride during the warm June summer. The plane unexpectedly stalled and crashed to the ground. Her cousin's legs were crushed and Robinson appeared to be lifeless. The man who found her among the wreckage took her to a mortician rather than the hospital, thinking that she was already gone. They soon realized she was still alive and rushed her to the hospital.

Miraculously, Robinson survived. But her arm was shattered, and one of her legs was broken in three places. The doctors were unsure if she would ever walk again. She was sent home in a wheelchair and remained there for the next six months, unable to walk. It would take a full two years for her to walk normally again. That young, enthusiastic track phenom had hit the lowest point in her life. She didn't even want to get out of bed, let alone think about running again.

Her dream of returning to the Olympics seemed impossible. Eventually she was able to walk and even run again, but her left leg could not bend like before. She was incapable of getting into the starting blocks for a 100m dash.

As the months and years went on, the joy within Betty's heart started to return with a hopeful realization. She couldn't run out of the starting blocks for the 100m, but she could remain upright as a runner in the 4x100m relay. She had won a silver medal as a member of the 1928 Olympic relay team. If she trained hard enough, she might earn a spot again on the American 4x100m team for the 1936 Olympics.

With renewed drive, Robinson trained hard for her chance to win another gold. Many other young female athletes were competing for the spot and able to pay for their own travel to the games. Robinson had to sell every piece of her 1928 Olympic memorabilia (besides her gold medal) in order to pay her way to Berlin for the Olympics. With enough money and a good qualifying time on the track, the American team welcomed the gold medalist to the team again.

The *New York Times* gave her the nickname "Smiling Betty" leading up to the Olympics. Her positive attitude was unmatched despite the doubt surrounding the American chances to win gold in the relay. The Germans were heavily favored and set a world record in the 4x100m relay qualifying round.

As the finals began, German Chancellor Adolf Hitler stood with confident cheers as his German team took an early lead in the race. The Germans had previously posted a time that was half a second faster than any other team on the track. It looked as though the medal was theirs for the taking.

As Betty Robinson took the baton in the third leg of the relay, the American team's hopes for a gold seemed to be slipping away. The Germans had overtaken the American team during the second leg of the relay. Robinson remained a distant second as they rounded the turn for the final handoff.

The German team seemed all alone in the front of the pack when the unexpected happened. The Germans fumbled the exchange and dropped the baton. Robinson passed her baton successfully to teammate Helen Stephens, whose long, strong stride carried the team across the finish line in first place. Hitler, meanwhile, sat down in disappointment as the Americans upset the Germans to win gold.

Betty Robinson, who couldn't walk five years earlier, had made her comeback. She was a gold medalist once again. Her smile had never been more deserved.

REFLECTION QUESTIONS

What helps you run and compete with a smile like "Smiling Betty" Robinson?

In what ways could Betty Robinson's story inspire someone struggling with an injury today?

What is the biggest challenge you have overcome as an athlete?

ROGER BANNISTER

SET IMPOSSIBLE GOALS

Running a mile in under four minutes seemed like an impossible feat in the middle of the 20th century. No one had ever been able to do it, but some potential milers were getting close. Among them a young medical student from England seemed the least likely to break the record.

Roger Bannister loved cross country as a kid and won a number of meets as a teenager. As World War II raged on in Europe, young Bannister was accepted into college at the age of 15. He arrived at Exeter College in Oxford as a 17-year-old medical student. He planned to focus on academics and run on the side when he had time. He didn't even own a pair of proper running spikes at the time.

Nevertheless, he continued to study, train, and compete well in middle distance races as a student-athlete. He was a potential candidate for England's 1948 Olympic team, but decided he wasn't ready to compete at that level yet. As he watched the 1948 games on TV, however, he realized his inner desire to become an Olympic athlete. So he set a goal to compete in the next Olympic Games.

Bannister dedicated a much greater amount of time to training during the next four years. With an increased amount of interval training, he was able to bring his mile time down under 4 minutes and 10 seconds, and his 800m down to 1:50. He entered the 1952 Olympics as one of the favorites for the 1500m run, but lost in a close race that wasn't decided until the last few meters. Although he set a new British record and ran faster than the old Olympic record, he still placed fourth in the race that day.

Bannister was crushed by the defeat. Was it better just to give up? He spent the next two months deciding whether to continue running or focus his full attention back on his studies. There were many other athletes repeatedly running faster than him. Could he continue to improve at the same rate as the other talented athletes?

Instead of backing down, Bannister set his sights on an even higher goal. He wanted to become the first man in history to run a four-minute mile. Many other men had come close in the 1940s and 1950s, some even within a couple of seconds of the barrier. Bannister knew that if he wanted to make history, he had to train hard and make his attempt soon before someone else took the record first.

He made his first attempt at the four-minute mile in 1953, but fell short by three seconds. His determination was unabated. He knew the four-minute mile was in reach after that race. He tried again a month later but missed the mark by two seconds and still a second slower than the reigning world record. Looking at the other times throughout the world, Bannister knew he had one final attempt before someone achieved the milestone.

It was windy and raining on the morning of May 6, 1954 in Oxford, England. Fortunately, the weather improved by the afternoon. Roger Bannister was ready to make a highly publicized attempt at the four-minute mile. Nearly 3,000 spectators came to watch and BBC radio broadcasted the event live.

The race began at 6:00pm. Bannister was accompanied by two men—future gold medalists Chris Brasher and Christopher Chataway—who would help set his pace. Brasher ran in front of the pack for the first two laps with Bannister clocking in with splits at 58 seconds and 1:58 respectively. Then Brasher backed down and Chataway moved to the front for the third lap. Bannister crossed the line at 3:01 with one lap to go. Bannister knew he would need to run the final 400m in under 60 seconds to break the record.

He passed Chataway after the first turn. His many years of interval training paid off and he increased his speed, giving everything he had left in the final 300m. Bannister later described the last few seconds of his run as "never ending." He leaped through the finishing tape and collapsed into a crowd of people with cheers and applause all around.

Bannister didn't need to hear the time to know that he had done it. The crowd erupted in cheers when the announcer started to read the time with the word "three." No one could hear the rest of the time. There was too much excitement in the stadium. Roger Bannister had done it. He had become the first man to run a mile in under four minutes. He had narrowly accomplished the feat, with a time of 3 minutes, 59.4 seconds.

It only took 46 days for his record to be broken. A year later, three other men broke the barrier in a single race. Since 1954, nearly 2,000 men have run a mile in under four minutes. The impossible became feasible thanks to Roger Bannister's great achievement.

A year after breaking the record, Bannister finally decided to retire from athletics and turn his full attention to medicine. He became a doctor and a very successful neurologist. Medicine and family became his sole passions, yet his name will be remembered throughout history for a once-thought impossible feat.

REFLECTION QUESTIONS

How did goal-setting help motivate Roger Bannister to continue to improve?

Roger Bannister had aspirations outside of athletics. What are some of your academic and career goals?

What is your biggest goal right now? How could you make it so big that it feels almost impossible to achieve?

EMIL ZÁTOPEK

RUN YOUR OWN RACE

At 16 years old, Emil Zátopek was working in a factory in his home country of Czechoslovakia when the sports coach picked him and a few other kids to run in an upcoming local race. He resisted at first, saying he wasn't a very good athlete. After a quick physical, though, he was cleared to run with no excuses. As the race began, he realized he might as well try to win. He ran hard and finished second out of one hundred kids.

Zátopek was immediately hooked. He wanted to become a winning runner. Despite modest living conditions at home, he joined the local athletics club. His family didn't have enough money to send him to fancy schools or training programs, so he studied other European athletes and created his own training program.

In 1944, Zátopek set national records in multiple distance events. He joined the army at the end of World War II and was able to train as both a soldier and a runner while he was enlisted. He qualified for the 1946 European Championships, then began to prepare for the 1948 Olympics.

Zátopek had big dreams and an uncanny work ethic. He was known to run in rain or snow, sometimes wearing multiple layers and even snow boots to complete his workouts. He pushed himself to the very limits every time he laced up his shoes.

He started to develop a unique training style. Since he didn't compete in an elite training facility, he relied instead on grit and determination. "An athlete cannot run with money in his pockets," he once said. "He must run with hope in his heart and dreams in his head."

Zátopek adopted the interval training method, which was not yet popular at the time. Instead of focusing only on mileage and long distances like the other great runners in the world, Emil ran high-speed intervals of 400m at a time, with 100m jogs to rest. He would do as many as 100 sets of 400m intervals in a single workout. These interval workouts trained his body to run at a faster pace than a normal long run. Many people called him a fool for his training method, but after he started winning races they began calling him a genius instead.

In his 1948 Olympic debut, he won gold in the 10,000m, and fell short of the win in the 5,000m. In that second race he ran with the leaders through pouring rain and mud until the final sprint to the finish. He passed the third and second-place runners to win silver just behind the gold medalist.

Zátopek went on to win multiple European Championships in distance events. He set and broke his own world records in the 5k and 10k that year, as well as in longer distances. His greatest feat, however, was another four years away.

In the 1952 Olympics, Zátopek first took gold again in the 10,000m, setting a new Olympic record. Then he had a chance to win his first gold in the 5,000m after the great disappointment in that race at the previous Olympics. He came from behind again, this time running a 57-second final lap to pass the three leading runners, which included Chris Chataway from Great Britain, who later helped runner Roger Bannister become the first person to run the four-minute mile. Zátopek set a new Olympic record in the 5,000m and took to the podium with another gold medal.

This alone was an incredible accomplishment. He could have gone home happy and proud of what he had done. Instead, on a whim, he decided he would compete in the Olympic marathon as well. He had never run in a marathon before. He hadn't been training for it either. No one had ever won gold in the marathon after winning gold in the other two distance events.

Zátopek would later say, "If you want to run, run a mile. If you want to experience a different life, run a marathon." He had a simple strategy in the race. He would run with the leader, worldrecord holder Jim Peters. As they ran, Zátopek would attempt to beat Peters not only physically, but mentally as well.

Zátopek wasn't known for the best running form. In fact, he was given the nickname "Czech Locomotive" and "Emil the Terrible" for his painful facial expressions and heavy breathing while he ran. Try to imagine the mental distraction Peters experienced with Zátopek wheezing and grunting along behind him. About halfway through the race, Zátopek asked Peters how he thought the race was going. When Peters responded that he thought it was "slow," Zátopek increased his pace and ran well ahead of the world record holder. Not long afterwards, Peters dropped out of the race with intense cramping.

The Czech Locomotive returned to the Helsinki Olympic Stadium as the sole leader in the race. He was well ahead of the next competitor, with a lead of about two minutes. Still grimacing with his awkward stride, Emil the Terrible did the unthinkable. He not only won his first marathon, he won Olympic gold and set a new Olympic record in the event. He became the only man to win gold in the 5k, 10k, and marathon in the same Olympics.

From then on Emil Zátopek was seen as a role model by other distance runners. He was well-known for his kindness and sense of humor. Although he didn't invent interval training, his success showed the need to supplement long runs with shorter distances at high speeds. He transformed long distance training and did so with a laugh and a smile—that is, at least when he wasn't running.

REFLECTION QUESTIONS

How did Emil Zátopek surprise those who doubted his training and ability?

In what ways can you develop your own extreme training routine?

In what ways have you outworked opponents or teammates?

WILMA RUDOLPH

OVERCOME EXPECTATIONS

Wilma Rudolph had everything stacked against her. She was born well before the normal term of a pregnancy in a small town just outside of Clarksville, Tennessee, north of Nashville. She grew up as a small and sickly child, suffering through pneumonia, scarlet fever, and polio all before the age of five. The polio severely damaged her legs, and she had to wear braces for support so she could.

Rudolph was the 20th child of 22 children in a large African American family, and she didn't have access to the finest medical attention. But her mother was determined to see to her recovery. She drove Wilma 50 miles south to Nashville once a week, sometimes taking the bus, to meet with doctors and physical therapists. Wilma's siblings helped massage her legs and motivated her to move without her braces (even though she wasn't supposed to do that).

At 12 she was finally able to prove to the doctors (and her mother) that she could walk without braces. That year, she set her sights on a big dream. She wanted to show her older siblings, the neighborhood kids, and her school's coaches that there was something special inside of her. She decided she was going to be a star on her school's basketball team.

She tried to get the middle school basketball coach's attention, but she was small and not nearly as good as her classmates. Wilma was determined to get the coach to help her. She wore her gym clothes beneath her street clothes so that she could be the first person in the gym during workouts. The coach still didn't seem to notice her, though. She wrote down and rehearsed a speech for the coach and approached him one day before practice. "What do you want?" he asked. Trying to remember the speech she had rehearsed all morning, Rudolph finally blurted out, "If you give me 10 minutes of your time, I will make a world-class athlete." The coach laughed hysterically, but he agreed to give her those 10 minutes.

Wilma worked hard each day. Outside of the gym, she convinced the neighborhood boys to show her some tips on becoming a better basketball player. When it was finally time to post the list of players for the team, the coach didn't call Rudolph's name. Devastated, she ran home crying, but the coach arrived at her house before she did. He was sitting down, talking to Rudolph's dad. He didn't come to talk about Wilma, though, he wanted Rudolph's older sister Yvonne on the team. Thankfully, their father knew of Wilma's dream. He told the coach, "If Yvonne is on the basketball team, then Wilma is on your basketball team also."

Rudolph wanted to be the best. Her hard work paid off and she finally earned a spot as a starter when she got to high school. She even broke the high school record for most points in a single season as a sophomore. But she still felt she had something to prove. She didn't know it yet, but basketball was about to open the doors to a completely different sport.

She earned the nickname "Skeeter," short for "mosquito," from her high school basketball coach because she was so quick on the court. Tennessee State University track coach Ed Temple happened to see her playing basketball one day. Noticing her speed, he asked if she would like to join his summer track camp for high schoolers. She was 14 years old and agreed to give it a try.

Two years later, after numerous AAU track championships, she earned a spot on the 1956 Olympic track team. Only a junior in high school, she was set to run the third leg of the 4x100m relay. The team, which included three other girls training under Coach Temple from TSU, earned a respectable third-place finish.

Rudolph arrived home with her bronze medal, ready to show to everyone who had ever doubted her just how special she was. The whole school—even the kids she didn't like—welcomed her with a big sign and an assembly of cheers. She passed around her bronze medal so everyone could see. When she finally got it back, she saw fingerprints all over it. They were the fingerprints of all the kids she had wanted to impress. She tried to wipe them off, but a bronze medal can't be shined. If it had been a gold medal, she could have wiped those fingerprints right off.

She decided in that moment to make it back to the Olympics in 1960. She enrolled in TSU as a student, continuing under Coach Temple's guidance and qualifying for the 100m and 200m races, as well as the 4x100m relay. She earned gold in all three events, becoming the first woman to win three gold medals in a single Olympic Games. Since the Olympics were televised that year, Wilma Rudolph became a national celebrity. No one had any doubt that Rudolph was special. She overcame all the odds, and, with the help of some loving parents and supportive coaches, she became the fastest woman in the world.

REFLECTION QUESTIONS

What do you think motivated Wilma Rudolph to set such impossible goals?

Are there other sports that led you to or away from track & field?

To whom would you most like to prove you can succeed?

JACKIE JOYNER-KERSEE

SHOW YOUR VERSATILITY

Jackie Joyner lost her first middle-school race. She not only lost, she came in dead last. She loved it anyway. She tasted the joy that comes through competition on the track.

Years later, Joyner would win multiple gold medals in the Olympics and multiple lifetime achievement awards. But as a child, Joyner was just one of the average girls on the track team. In 1976 she sat on the living-room floor with her older brother Al, watching the summer Olympic Games. She saw a 19-year-old girl from the United States named Evelyn Ashford run in the 100m and 200m races. Joyner was amazed to see someone like herself, another young black woman, compete on the world stage.

In that moment, at 14 years old, Joyner decided she wanted to be an Olympic athlete. She went to her track coach and told him she wanted to be in the Olympics. With some surprise, he explained to her the kind of dedication and hard work needed to compete at that level. She was ready for the challenge.

Joyner started to train even harder than before. She ran with her track team in the park, since their school didn't have a track. She built her own long jump pit in their front yard, borrowing some sand from the playground across the street. In her free time she practiced jumping into that pit.

She came to understand an important lesson at a young age: if she put in the work, she could decrease her running times by just one tenth of a second (and a half-inch more as a jumper). Little by little, she made improvements and got stronger and faster. She saw the difference between the kids at track meets earning ribbons for fourth through eighth place, and the top three standing on the podiums with medals. She had to figure out how to become one of those winners.

Joyner had not yet proven herself as the renowned athlete that she was destined to become. That began to change when she discovered another inspirational woman in a TV movie. Mildred Ella "Babe" Didrikson Zaharias won two gold medals and one silver in the 1932 Olympics. Before that, "Babe" led her semi-professional basketball team to a national championship. After her Olympic success, she decided to take up golf and compete in the LPGA. She went on to win 48 tournaments, including the U.S. Open.

Using Babe Zaharias as her inspiration, Joyner decided to set herself apart as a multi-event and multi-sport athlete. She expanded her focus on basketball during the winter and the pentathlon during her spring high school years. Her pentathlons in track featured five events: 100m hurdles, high jump, long jump, shot put, and the 800m run. She went on to win four pentathlon titles in high school and earn a scholarship to play basketball at UCLA.

Jackie was a four-year starter for the UCLA basketball team, but she took a year off from basketball to compete in the 1984 Summer Olympics. Despite a lingering hamstring injury, Jackie earned a silver medal in the heptathlon. Joining her on that Olympic team was Evelyn Ashford, the sprinter Joyner had idolized in the 1976 Olympics. Ashford went on to win two gold medals in 1984. Also on the team that year was Joyner's older brother Al, who earned the gold medal in the men's triple jump.

Silver medalist Joyner wasn't done yet. She continued to train under her UCLA coach Bob Kersee. After a romance developed, they got married in 1986 and she began hyphenating her name as Joyner-Kersee. She returned for the 1988 Olympics, earning gold medals in both the heptathlon and long jump. Joyner-Kersee set a world record that still remains today with 7,291 total points in the heptathlon (100m hurdles, high jump, shot put, 200m, long jump, javelin throw, and 800m run). She won gold again in the 1992 heptathlon and bronze in the long jump. She went on to win many more world championships during her spectacular career.

Joyner-Kersee earned the highest honor in track, the Jesse Owens Award, in back-to-back years in 1986 and 1987. In 2013 that same award was renamed in her honor for all female winners as the Jackie Joyner-Kersee Award. Sports Illustrated voted her the Greatest Female Athlete of All-Time, just one spot ahead of one of her greatest inspirations, Babe Didrikson Zaharias.

REFLECTION QUESTIONS

What are your favorite sports to compete in, and why?

Who are the athletes on TV that inspire you the most, and why?

In what ways does Jackie Joyner-Kersee's story inspire you as an athlete?

FLORENCE GRIFFITH JOYNER

WIN WITH STYLE

Florence Griffith Joyner not only became the fastest female sprinter ever recorded, she did so with an absolutely unique style. Born as the seventh of 11 children in Los Angeles, California, Florence grew up in relative poverty in public housing. She played sports against her older brothers and soon discovered a talent as a sprinter. She joined a local track organization and won the Jesse Owens National Youth Games when she was 14 years old.

Florence would later enter college at California State University at Northridge, then win a national title under coach Bob Kersee. Despite the success in college, she had to drop out to provide financial support for her family, taking a job as a bank teller. Coach Kersee transferred to UCLA and found scholarship money to pay for Florence to go back to school. She went on to earn a degree in psychology and experienced enough success on the track to be in contention for the Olympics.

When Evelyn Ashford dropped out of the 200m Olympic Trials in 1984, Florence was able to secure the spot as a sprinter and won a silver medal. It was an impressive achievement, but not enough for her to make a living. Track did not have enough endorsement money at the time to enable her to become a professional athlete. After the Olympics, she returned home to her job as a bank teller, supplementing her income by styling hair and nails to help support her family.

While struggling to make ends meet, she wondered how to make a return to the world stage on the track. The more she thought about it, the more she realized that it wasn't enough just to win. She had to win with style. If she wanted to earn any income in endorsement deals, she had to make a splash.

Growing up, Griffith Joyner loved fashion and cultivated a unique style. Other kids teased her for the way she wore her hair or the way she came to school with different colored pairs of socks. She combined her passion for fashion with her love of running and experimented early in her career designing distinctive track uniforms.

She plotted her return to the Olympics with a combined focus on skill and style. She married her long-time boyfriend, Al Joyner, brother of storied Olympian Jackie Joyner-Kersee, and brother-in-law to coach Bob Kersee from UCLA. Coach Kersee trained with Florence two days a week while her husband became her coach for the other three days. Eventually, Al became her sole coach.

By this time she took on a new identity. She was no longer "Florence Griffith Joyner," she was now going by the nickname "Flo-Jo." She was unmistakable on the track. She wore makeup and sported long, flowing hair and six-and-a-half-inch nails intricately designed with gold medals or the Stars and Stripes. She became known for her "one-legger," tights that covered only one leg with bright bathing-suit-style bottoms.

"Dress good to look good. Look good to feel good. And feel good to run fast!" That was her motto. That is exactly what she did in the 1988 Olympic Trials. Not only did she become the fastest woman ever to run the 100m dash with a time of 10.49 seconds, she did so with unmistakable flair. With her hair, long nails, and a purple "one-legger," Flo-Jo made history. She went on to win gold medals in the 100m, 200m, and 4x100m relay in the Olympics.

Her hard work and dedication finally paid off after that 1988 Olympic Games. She became a celebrity and fashion icon. She earned millions of dollars in endorsement deals. She even had a Barbie doll made in her honor with her signature "one-legger." Her sister-in-law, Jackie Joyner-Kersee, later said that Flo-Jo "took track & field off the sports page to the front page" of the newspaper.

Sadly, 10 years after her Olympic victories, Flo-Jo died unexpectedly in her sleep due to complications of an epileptic seizure. Her legacy lives on as one of the first track & field athletes to transcend the sport. Her sense of fashion and style would inspire generations of sprinters to stand out in both skill and signature appearances.

REFLECTION QUESTIONS

What is or could be your signature style?

How do you stand out on and off the track?

How have you helped your family when they needed you the most, as Flo-Jo did for her parents and siblings?

DICK FOSBURY

CREATE YOUR OWN TECHNIQUE

From a spectator's point of view, the second-place finish in the 1965 Oregon high school state championship in the high jump probably wasn't noteworthy. Dick Fosbury's jump of 6 feet 5.5 inches was respectable, but not the best in the state that year. The notable thing about that achievement, however, is the way Fosbury won the silver medal. He had a different approach. Everyone else in the field jumped upright with legs looking like scissors or dove sideways with arms and leg extended over the bar. But Fosbury made his jump by leaping over the pole backwards.

A year earlier, a local newspaper shared a photo of young Dick Fosbury's unique form with a caption, "Fosbury Flops Over Bar." Dick's experimental technique in the high jump had a name for the first time: the "Fosbury Flop." Originally, Dick used the traditional techniques his coaches taught him. But the scissors method and straddle method never worked for the 6ft, 5in teenager. So he started to experiment. At first, his coaches tried to get him to focus on the old way of doing things. When he broke the school record as a junior, however, they let him do it his own way.

The goal of the high jump is to leap over a bar without knocking it down and land on the other side. The only other rule is that jumpers must lift off with one foot. In the early years, the high jump pit where jumpers landed was made of sand or wood chips. As Fosbury tried new ways of getting over the bar, the wood chips were being replaced by foam pads. Fosbury and others could now land on their backs instead of their feet after jumping over the bar.

His high school success earned him a spot on Oregon State's track team. At first his college coaches discouraged his experiments just as his high school coaches had done before. Fosbury had to use the traditional straddle method, but was allowed to experiment in freshmen track meets if he wanted. History repeated itself again when Fosbury cleared 6 feet 10 inches to break the school record using his Fosbury Flop. Afterwards, his college coach began filming Fosbury's method so he could teach it to younger athletes.

With the 1968 Summer Olympics coming up soon, Dick Fosbury had a chance to demonstrate his unique form on an international stage. After winning the NCAA national championship in the high jump he qualified for the Olympic team. By this time he had perfected the Fosbury Flop with a J-shaped approach to the bar that generated just enough momentum to give him an extra boost over the bar.

Dick Fosbury not only won the gold medal in 1968, he also set an Olympic record with a jump of 7 feet 4 1/4 inches.

Most people had never seen anything like it before. Every other medalist before Fosbury had used the scissors or straddle method. Every other athlete in that year's Olympics used the traditional method as well. His win spread a shockwave through the event and single-handedly changed the high jump forever.

The gold medalist in the women's high jump in the following Olympics in 1972 used the Fosbury Flop. A total of 28 out of 40 male high jumpers that year used Fosbury's method as well. Almost every medalist since 1972 has used the Flop to succeed in the high jump.

Dick Fosbury returned to Oregon State to win another NCAA title after the Olympics. He graduated and worked in civil engineering and politics in the years after his athletic career. Fosbury easily earned his place in the Track and Field Hall of Fame in 1981. He must have looked with pride on each of the Olympic Games after 1972, seeing men and women use a little experimental form he tried out in high school. He had the courage to try something new and changed his sport in the process.

REFLECTION QUESTIONS

What are the traditional methods in your event?

What are some experiments you can do to create your own unique style?

In what ways have you set an example for other athletes?

STEVE PREFONTAINE

BECOME A LEGEND

Professional sports are an integral part of American culture. The United States is the birthplace of baseball, basketball, and American football. These sports have dominated media and made millions of dollars for athletes, coaches, and owners alike. When most young people grow up wanting to play team sports, they gravitate toward professional football, basketball, or baseball.

Like most of his peers in the 1960s, Steve Prefontaine wanted to play football and basketball in middle school. Cross country and track were not very popular at the time. Adults didn't compete in marathons by the thousands, and few people ran at all for fitness or fun. The running boom of the 1970s was still a decade away. Long-distance runners needed a hero to look up to, and they would find one in the legendary Steve "Pre" Prefontaine.

But back in 1964, the thought of running on a team for competition didn't occur to young Prefontaine. It didn't matter that he was short and rarely saw the football field or the basketball court. He didn't think much of the cross-country team running past the football field during fall practice in his eighth-grade year. But later that semester, when he started to show promise during some long-distance training in his P.E. class, Prefontaine started to think differently about running.

Instead of football, he went out for the cross-country team as a freshman at Marshfield High School in Oregon. By the end of the first season, Prefontaine had worked his way up to become the second-fastest runner on the roster. He placed 53rd in the state and got his mile time in track down to 5:01. After a fairly unimpressive sophomore year, his coach convinced him to train harder during the summer before his junior year. Something clicked. In the fall of 1967, Prefontaine went undefeated in every cross country meet and won the state title. He continued to train harder, and went undefeated in cross country again the following year. He set the high school national record in track with a time of 8:41.5 in the 2-mile run.

Prefontaine was the most highly recruited high school distance runner in the country, but he only wanted to go to one school: the University of Oregon. Renowned track coach Bill Bowerman wanted Prefontaine, too, and promised to make him one of the greatest distance runners in the world. Bowerman was a legend. Not only did he co-found the shoe company Nike with Phil Knight, he also popularized jogging as a fitness activity. More than a decade before Prefontaine's success, Bowerman published a bestselling book titled *Jogging* that sparked interest in running for fun and competition. The book was successful, but running still needed an icon to add fuel to the movement's fire.

That fire turned into an inferno with the arrival of Prefontaine at the University of Oregon. His immediate success in track and cross country was accompanied by local and national fame. He was now affectionately called "Pre" by his fans, who brought signs to meets that read "Legend," "Go Pre," and sarcastically, "Stop Pre." By 1970 he was on the cover of *Sports Illustrated*. After multiple NCAA titles, he qualified for the 1972 Olympics and won the 5,000m trials before placing fourth in the finals.

Prefontaine came home to finish his final year as a collegiate athlete and look to the future with renewed vigor. Between 1973 and 1975, he set American records in the 2-mile, 3-mile, 6-mile, 2,000m, 3,000m, 5,000m, and 10,000m. He broke these and his own records 14 times.

Sadly, tragedy came just one year before his return to the Olympics. After winning another 5,000m race on May 29, 1975, Prefontaine went out to a party with some fellow Olympic athletes. On his way home down a narrow road near the University of Oregon's campus, Prefontaine's car jumped the curb and flipped over. He was pronounced dead at the scene.

The sudden death spread shockwaves across the running community. The running boom of the 1970s was underway and Prefontaine was one of the most famous runners in America. Generations of long-distance runners would look to him for inspiration. In 1995, a documentary of his life titled *Fire on the Track* was released. And his life was made into two movies 20 years after his death—*Prefontaine* in 1997 and *Without Limits* in 1998. His story motivated generations of young athletes to trade in dreams of football, baseball, or basketball fame for success on the track and cross country teams instead.

REFLECTION QUESTIONS

What do you love most about running?

Have you ever felt your size held you back? Why or why not?

What lesson can you learn from Steve Prefontaine's death?

CARL LEWIS

LEAVE YOUR OWN LEGACY

As the head coach of his alma mater's track & field team at the University of Houston, Carl Lewis meets with every athlete and asks: "Where do you want to be when you turn 40?" The answer doesn't have to be about sports. In fact, most of the time it deals with something outside of track. Based on the answer, coach Lewis works with the young athletes to make a plan to build their own personal legacy.

When Lewis turned 40, he had been named the "Sportsman of the Century" by the International Olympic Committee. His many great feats include nine gold medals in the Olympics and 10 world championships. He was an iconic figure in track & field for nearly two decades.

If a coach had asked a teenage Lewis to describe where he wanted to be at the age of 40, his goals for success might have seemed impossible. As a college athlete at Houston, Lewis showed a lot of promise. His primary focus at the time was the long jump. He broke the high school national record in 1979, then went on to win the NCAA championship with a jump of 27ft 4 1/2in. With the 1980 U.S.

boycott of the Olympics, Lewis would have another four years to decide what legacy he was going to leave.

In college he showed some additional potential beyond the long jump. He ran on the 4x100m national relay team and ranked seventh in the 100m dash in the world. Still, he was known mostly as a long jumper at the time.

When the 1984 Olympics came around, everyone looked to Lewis to break the longstanding world record in the long jump. Did he want to become known as the world record holder in the long jump? Sure, but Lewis had his sights on a different legacy. Almost 50 years earlier, the great Jesse Owens made history by winning four gold medals in the Olympics, the 100m, 200m, 4x100m relay, and long jump. Carl Lewis wanted to make history as the second person to accomplish that feat.

First, Lewis won gold in the 100m dash, breaking the 10 seconds with a 9.99s mark. Next came the long jump. He was the heavy favorite. The media had built him up as the man to beat the world record of 29ft 2 1/4in, which had been set 16 years earlier. With a roaring crowd in the Los Angeles Coliseum, Lewis made a spectacular first jump of 28ft even. It was the first of six possible attempts he could make. Lewis scratched his second attempt and then chose not to make another jump so he could save his body for the 200m qualifying and final round the next day. He believed he could easily win gold with his first jump, so he didn't make another attempt. Surprisingly, Lewis was met with boos from the crowd, who thought he was being a quitter.

Lewis won the 200m gold medal the next day and then went on to win his fourth gold as the anchor of the world-record-setting 4x100m relay team. He had done it. He had matched Jesse Owens's great accomplishment and won four gold medals in a single Olympic Games.

The response from the media and the public was not what Lewis expected. People felt he lacked humility. He was flashy and enjoyed the media attention. Other athletes criticized him for being arrogant, and a negative reputation began to form around his persona. Instead of earning endorsements from big brands after the Olympics, he actually lost deals with Nike and Coca-Cola. He was at the top of the sport, yet failed to earn the respect he felt he deserved. Was this his legacy?

He was only 23 years old at the time. It was only his first Olympics. How far could he take his career from there? Where could he be at the age of forty?

Carl Lewis returned to the Olympics four years later. Although he came in second place during the 100m race, the winner ended up testing positive for steroid use. So, Lewis was awarded the gold medal (and the world record time of 9.92s) instead. That year he also became the first person to defend a title in the long jump, winning gold with a leap of 28ft 7 1/4in. Rising star Mike Powell, from the United States, finished just short of Lewis's best jump.

Carl Lewis and Mike Powell met again in the 1991 World Championships in what may remain the greatest long jump competition in history. Both men had the potential to break the world record in the long jump. Lewis had won 65 straight competitions in the long jump at that time, never losing to Powell.

Lewis had the top jump in the qualifying round leading up to the storied final. Lewis took the lead in the final with his first jump, while Powell's first attempt was at the bottom of the group of eight competitors. Powell's second attempt still didn't match Lewis, who went on to jump a personal best of 28ft 11 1/2in (8.83m) with his wind-aided third attempt. Powell fouled his next attempt. And then Lewis made history. Although it was wind-aided, he surpassed the world record with a jump of 29ft 2 3/4in. The record couldn't count for the history books because of the wind, but it put him in first place in the competition.

Powell had two attempts left. The wind died down and he made his first sprint down the runway with a perfect liftoff and landing to jump 8.95m (29ft 4 1/4in). He became the new official world record holder and moved up to first place in the event. Lewis's attempts to defeat Powell's jump fell just short of the record. His final two jumps in that competition reached beyond 29ft and remain in the top five overall in history. Still, Powell won with a jump distance that has never been matched.

Carl Lewis was 30 years old. What would his legacy be now? Powell was the new top long jumper. Michael Johnson was the new world record holder in the 200m. Lewis won gold in the long jump again in the 1992 Olympics—defeating Powell—and continued to anchor the 4x100m relay team, but failed to qualify in either the 100m or 200m.

Four more years passed and in 1996 Lewis had the chance to win a gold medal in the long jump for an incredible fourth Olympics in a row. Powell was suffering from a leg injury, while Lewis was feeling healthy.

Lewis did it. With a jump of 27ft 10 1/2in, he won gold again. It was his ninth gold medal. That put him in a tie for the second-most Olympic gold medals of all time, behind only super swimmer Michael Phelps. Lewis decided to officially retire from track & field the next year.

As the new millennium began, Carl Lewis could look back on his career with pride in his legacy. He was never able to hold the world record in his main event, the long jump, but his long-lasting career solidified his place as a track & field legend. He defended his long jump title in four consecutive Olympics and matched Jesse Owens's feat of four gold medals in a single Olympic Games.

REFLECTION QUESTIONS

Where do you want to be when you turn 40?

What would you like your legacy to be on the track?

What would you like your legacy to be off the track?

MICHAEL JOHNSON

EARN YOUR REPUTATION

During his long and historic career, Michael Johnson has accumulated many nicknames. With his multiple gold medals as a sprinter, he has been hailed as the "World's Fastest Human." He made history in the Olympics by wearing custom-made, iconic spikes of shiny gold and was afterwards called the "Man with the Golden Shoes." His career was so impressive for so many years that he was even given the name "Superman" by his admirers.

But he also went by a less complimentary nickname: "The Duck." Johnson had a unique, upright running style with a short stride. He ran with supreme control over his body, but he never fit the mold of a textbook sprinter. Every college recruiter that spoke to Johnson during his high school years encouraged him to adjust his form. Only Coach Clyde Hart from Baylor University was willing to let him maintain the upright running style, but even he later admitted that no one expected Michael Johnson to become a superstar.

During his college years, Johnson sparked and solidified Baylor's reputation as "Quarter Mile U" under Coach Hart for their success in the 400m run (one quarter of a mile). As a member of the 4x400m relay team, Johnson won two NCAA championships. He also showed shocking success in the 200m, breaking the university's school record and winning three national championships in the event. He finished college with a business degree in accounting and turned his focus on becoming a full-time sprinter.

The 200m and 400m combination was odd at the time. Sprinters usually ran the 100m or the 200m along with the 4x100m relay. The 400m runners usually stuck to the 400m and the 4x400 relay. Johnson, however, chose to defy the odds and run in both events. Could "The Duck" really find success across two running distances? Indeed, he did.

In the 1991 World Championships, he won the 200m, setting a course record of 20.01 seconds. He was the favorite to win the 200m in the 1992 Olympics in Barcelona, but he contracted food poisoning just before the semifinal race. He was able to rebuild enough strength to compete on the world-record breaking 4x400m relay team to win his first Olympic gold medal. He came home with a renewed focus on both events: 200m and 400m.

In 1993, Johnson won his first U.S. and world titles in the 400m and 4x400m relays. His split in the relay was a shocking 42.91 seconds, which has yet to be beaten on record. Then in 1995 he became the first male athlete to win the 200m and 400m double, then added the triple with a 4x400m relay win. This was only the beginning. He was about to make history in his return to the Olympics.

When Michael Johnson stepped onto the Atlanta track in 1996, he was wearing his custom-made Nike gold spikes. There was no doubt about his intentions. He was planning to win three gold medals. The way he did it, though, was incredible.

Remember, sprinters just didn't typically run both the 200m and the 400m. But Johnson tore that stereotype apart. At 28 years old, he ran the 200m during the Olympic Trials in a time of 19.66 seconds. That broke a world record that had stood for 17 years. But that wasn't even his most impressive feat. After easily winning gold in the 400m with a new Olympic record time of 43.49, Johnson returned to the track for the 200m final. No one had ever won both of these events in a single Olympics.

He lined up in lane three sporting his signature gold spikes and matching gold lace necklace. The race began and Johnson launched with a powerful start around the turn. By the time they reached the last 100m straight, Johnson had taken a heavy lead. Despite his short stride and upright form, Johnson continued to pull ahead with unrelenting focus on the finish line. Without even a lean across the line, Johnson looked to the side to see the result. Most records are broken by hundredths of a second and rarely as much as a tenth of a second. Michael Johnson broke his standing world record by a shocking .34 (three tenths of a second) with a time of 19.32 seconds, the largest improvement ever in a 200m world record. It has rightly been called one of the greatest feats in Olympic history.

Johnson tweaked a muscle in that spectacular race and didn't run in the winning 4x400 relay that year. He would return to the Olympics four years later to defend his title in the 400m and compete in the winning 4x400 relay (though the team was later disqualified for a teammate's drug use). Although he struggled with injuries during the years after 1996, he continued to defend his 400m title. He remained unbeaten for seven straight years and won 58 consecutive 400m races. All this from a man who defied stereotypes of running form and what it means to be a sprinter. Michael Johnson remains one of the greatest track & field athletes of all time.

REFLECTION QUESTIONS

What are some of your nicknames and how did you get them?

What makes your running style unique?

What are your favorite events to compete in and why?

PAULA RADCLIFFE

EXCEL IN THE RIGHT EVENT

Sometimes the difference between good and great is a mental shift from one event to another.

Paula Radcliffe was the most popular professional runner in Britain in the late 1990s. She found early success with a first-place finish in the Junior World Cross Country Championships and shifted into a promising professional career in the 3,000m, 5,000m, and 10,000m races. At the height of her cross country fame, however, she fell short of gold medals in the World Cross Country Championships. She had a couple of first-place finishes, but most of the time she was finishing between 5th and 2nd place in every event. With high hopes of winning the 2000 Sydney Olympics, she took an early lead only to fall back into a fourth-place finish by the end of the race.

The underwhelming finishes were capped off by an embarrassing moment on national television in 2001. Gary Lough, her husband and manager, berated her at the finish line for her fourth place finish. Radcliffe was in tears, but Lough was upset about her tactics during the race. He felt she should have attacked earlier in the competition. She reserved her kick until it was too late.

It was just another in a long line of impressive runs that fell short of greatness. Radcliffe had so much potential. Earlier in 2001 she did win the World Cross Country Championships in the Long Cross Country (7.7 km) event. Whether she realized it at the time or not, she was about to become one of the greatest long-distance runners in the history of the world. It all came from a simple change in her focus.

Paula Radcliffe began running at the age of seven when her father became a marathoner to get into shape. Sometimes he would take Paula on long runs through the woods. She enjoyed running and showed a lot of potential as a young girl. Her father wanted to encourage her to pursue running in competitions.

Radcliffe's father took her to see the London Marathon when she was about 10 years old. As an adult, she would recall how inspired she felt to see Ingrid Kristiansen win the race. A year later Kristiansen would set the world record in the London Marathon. Radcliffe remembered thinking, "I'd love to do that."

So, Radcliffe pursued competitive running by joining the Bedford & Country Athletics Club. Her father became the vice chairman and her mother managed the cross country team. Radcliffe was coached by Alex Stanton, who remained her coach from age 12 all the way through her professional career. She achieved early success, and her promise increased every year as she earned fame in Great Britain as a long-distance runner.

At the age of 29, however, Radcliffe realized she needed to make a change. Kristiansen had been an inspiration to her in the marathon at a young age. What if she could be that same kind of inspiration to someone else? So, in 2002 she planned to shift her focus to the marathon instead of the shorter cross country distances.

She ran her first London Marathon in 2002, 19 years after she witnessed the event for the first time. She not only won the race, she broke the course record and ran the second fastest time by a woman in history. Furthermore, the marathon training paid off in the shorter distances, too. Earlier that year she took a short break from the marathon training to compete in the World Cross Country Championships, defending her title to win the 10k again. She also took first place in the Commonwealth Games in the 5k and in the European Championships in the 10k that year.

But her real focus was on winning marathons. After her marathon debut in April of 2002, she went on to run the Chicago Marathon in October. There she set a new world record in the marathon with a time of 2:17:18. She wasn't finished. She returned again the next year to win the London Marathon and break her world record with a time of 2:15:25. That time would remain the world record in the marathon for the next 16 years!

Radcliffe wasn't just a long-distance runner; she was a marathoner. She became a three-time winner of the London Marathon, three-time winner of the New York City Marathon, and took additional marathon wins in Chicago and Vilamoura, Portugal.

Like Ingrid Kristiansen, Radcliffe went on to inspire young runners throughout the world. Also like Kristiansen, she took time off from running to become a mother in 2007 and 2010. She fought off injuries and continued to battle through to victories before finally retiring in 2015.

She earned multiple awards in Great Britain, including Sports Personality of the Year, Comeback of the Year, and World Athlete of the Year. Queen Elizabeth II made her a Member of the Order of the British Empire and in 2010 she was inducted into the England Athletics Hall of Fame. She became one of the most recognized names in all of running because of a shift in her identity to become a marathoner and one of the greatest marathoners that ever lived.

REFLECTION QUESTIONS

If you were to try another event in track & field, what would it be and why?

How would your training need to change to compete in a different event?

Who are the athletes today that inspire you the most?

USAIN BOLT

IGNORE EXPECTATIONS

With his eight Olympic gold medals and 11 world championships, Usain Bolt is justifiably called the greatest sprinter of all time. The Jamaican phenom holds world records in the 100m, 200m, and 4x100m relay and won gold in all three events in three consecutive Olympics (2008, 2012, 2016). He has been a track icon for nearly two decades.

Back in 2007, however, his potential was still only that: potential. Many people didn't believe in him. They doubted his work ethic and wrote off his success in his teenage years as just raw ability. Bolt had a history of having fun and playing practical jokes during training and even during meets. He loved dancing and playing video games. His favorite thing to eat was fast food, and he didn't take nutrition seriously as a teenager.

But the country of Jamaica had high hopes for Bolt. Although in his youth he wanted to play cricket or soccer, he showed unbelievable promise on the track. He took home multiple gold medals as a teenager, running the

200m and 400m individual events and 4x100m and 4x400m relays at high school and national junior championships. The prime minister of Jamaica took notice and encouraged him to train in the nation's capital city. His fame grew and so did the pressure to perform at a high level.

At 18 years old, Usain Bolt turned pro just in time for the 2004 Olympics. Despite high hopes of proving himself on the world stage, Bolt suffered a leg injury that led to his elimination during the prelims of the 200m. He continued to struggle with injuries in 2005 and 2006.

The disappointments came to a peak in 2007. He had hoped it would be his breakout year. At the World Championships in Osaka he faced off against rival Tyson Gay from the United States in the 200m. He ran a respectable 19.91s, but lost to Gay's 19.75s world championship record. The Jamaican 4x100 relay team also fell short with a silver medal behind the United States.

Usain Bolt came home with disappointing silver medals ready to make a change. His main focus in the early years as a professional was the 200m and 400m. He was following in the footsteps of U.S. star Michael Johnson, who set world records in those events. His coach Glenn Mills encouraged him to stick with the 400m. He knew that Bolt's uncommon 6ft 7in height as a sprinter would be a disadvantage. Long legs made it difficult for him to come out of the starting blocks quickly, giving other runners an edge in the shorter distances.

Bolt ignored these expectations. He wanted to become the fastest man in the world by competing in the 100m. He felt that his long legs would give him an advantage by producing longer than average strides. After the 2007 setbacks in the World Championships, Bolt became more serious than ever about his training. He ate well and trained six days a week. He finally convinced his coach that he should compete in the 100m after he broke the Jamaican record in the 200m, which had been held by the great Don Quarrie for 36 years.

In 2008, Usain Bolt wasn't the fastest 100m runner in the world; he wasn't even the fastest 100m runner in Jamaica. The world record was held by fellow 4x100m relay team-mate Asafa Powell, who consistently ran sub-10-second times in the 100m. Powell, not Bolt, ran against Tyson Gay in the 2007 World Championship 100m. But like Bolt, Powell fell short and came away with a bronze medal.

With the Olympics coming up in the summer of 2008, Bolt knew he had some work to do. He ignored criticism about his work ethic and diet. He still showed up to the track with jokes and a smile, but his antics were in the past. He was putting in the work behind the scenes and preparing himself for greatness.

His ambition was boosted on May 3, 2008 when he broke the 10-second barrier for the first time, running a 9.76—just behind Powell's 100m world record of 9.74. Despite his size, Bolt showed he had potential as a short-distance sprinter. He finally got his chance to show the world how fast he really was against rival U.S. sprinter Tyson Gay on May 31, 2008. It was only the fifth time Bolt had run the 100m as a professional. Gay seemed to be unbeatable at the time.

On May 31, 2008 both Bolt and Gay arrived at Icahn Stadium in New York City for the Reebok Grand Prix, ready to prepare the world for the upcoming Olympic matchup. Gay saw Jamaican Asafa Powell as his main rival in the 100m at the time, but Powell was recovering from an injury and didn't compete in the race. Bolt had shown some promising finishes, but Gay was the favorite to win.

With heavy rains and fog during the day, the race had to be postponed until later in the evening. The track was wet and the crowd was sparse. Under the stadium lights, Bolt lined up in lane 4 next to Tyson Gay in lane 5. The gun went off and Bolt took a surprising early lead right out of the starting blocks. He was expected to have a slow start, but he began well ahead of the field. Then with his long and comfortable stride he continued to edge out all of the other runners, even Gay. Bolt crossed the finish line with an incredible world-record time of 9.72 seconds.

Coach Glenn Mills said after the race, "This is just the beginning." Bolt went on to win gold in the 100m, 200m, and 4x100m in the 2008 Olympic Games. He finished the 100m Olympic finals with a shocking 9.69s and did so while slowing down and beating his chest to celebrate as he passed the finish line.

Was he falling back into his old habits, lacking seriousness about the sport? Not at all. Bolt celebrated his victories with his signature "Lighting Bolt" dance, but he backed up the show with performance on the track. He successfully completed the "triple-triple," winning gold in three events during three consecutive Olympic Games. He set and broke his own world records in the 100m, 200m, and 4x100m relay. He earned 19 *Guinness Book of World Records*, second only to Olympian Michael Phelps. He put in the work and rightfully earned his place as the fastest man in the world.

REFLECTION QUESTIONS

What expectations of both success and failure do you have to overcome?

How well do you balance fun with hard work?

Who are your biggest competitors right now, and how do they push you to train harder?

MO FARAH

MOTIVATE WITH MULTIPLE INSPIRATIONS

Mo Farah lined up among the fastest long-distance runners in the world to compete for the gold in the 10,000m run at the 2016 Olympic Games in Rio. He was there to defend his title as the gold medal winner in the 2012 Olympics. That year he had achieved the coveted "distance double," winning both the 5,000m and the 10,000m races. After four additional years of training, including European and world championships, Farah was ready to win again.

The race began exactly as planned. Farah ran in the crowded pack of distance runners near his training partner —top USA runner Galen Rupp. At the front ran the spectacular runners from the Ethiopian and Kenyan teams. But during the 10th lap, about halfway through the race, Farah tripped on Rupp's foot and rolled across the track. He was nearly stepped on as he scrambled to get up. Shaken and emotional, his hopes for another gold medal seemed to be fading away.

What would motivate a person to recover from that kind of setback? Fortunately for Farah, he was no stranger to adversity. In a 2022 documentary about his life, Farah revealed a very troubled childhood. He was born in Somalia in 1983 and separated from his family at the age of nine. He was kidnapped and sold into service in the United Kingdom and told to take the name Mohamed Farah instead of his birth name Hussein Abdi Kahin. There he was forced to work in a home essentially as a slave and forbidden to go to school until the age of 11 or 12.

When Farah was allowed to go to school, P.E. teacher Alan Watkinson noticed the young boy's athletic ability and encouraged him to run and play soccer. Eventually, Farah confided in Watkinson, telling his teacher about his living situation. Watkinson contacted social services to get him into a foster home.

With a new school and new caretakers, young Farah channeled all of his past trauma into running during his teenage years. By 2001 he had won his first junior championship in the 5000m. He became a professional distance runner at that point, moving in to live with a group of the top distance runners in the area. Every day they slept, ate, trained, and rested together. Before long, Farah was winning national titles and world championships leading up to his 2012 Olympic golds.

Before each race, Farah relied on his Islamic faith for inspiration. He said a personal prayer to Allah and read prayers of invocations called *duas*. He tried to live out the words of his holy book, the *Qur'an*, which said one should work hard at whatever they do.

Was it his childhood that motivated him? Was it his faith? Or did he run for the many coaches and training partners who helped him along the way? Probably, it was a combination of these experiences, plus one more as an adult.

As he got up from that accidental stumble in the 10,000m Olympic race in 2016, Farah had one thing on his mind. He had promised his stepdaughter Rihanna that he would bring home another gold. Farah recovered from the fall and sprinted back to his spot in the pack of runners. He returned to his original race strategy, continuing as planned. He made his way to the front of the pack, with the two Ethiopians on his heels. Now he trailed only the leading runner from Kenya. With a last burst of speed in the final 100m, Farah edged ahead of the Kenyan on the home stretch to take back the gold medal.

He went on to achieve the distance double again with a gold in the 5000m seven days later. "I did it for Rihanna. My daughter!! This is for my family," he posted on Instagram. He dedicated these and all of his gold medals to his children. Thanks to a loving wife and role-model father, all of Farah's kids—including Rihanna, twin daughters Aisha and Amani, and a son named Hussein who was only ten months old at the time—led a better childhood than Farah got to experience himself. They get to grow up seeing a motivated man draw from years of both adversity and support to achieve something spectacular.

REFLECTION QUESTIONS

Who are the coaches that have helped you along your journey?

How has religion played a role in your training and race preparation?

Who among your family motivates you and inspires you the most?

ALLYSON FELIX

INSPIRE OTHERS WITH PASSION

At 4:00am in the morning, Allyson Felix was training in the dark. It was October 2018 and 15 years into her professional career as a sprinter. Her work ethic was practically unmatched. She regularly had workouts six days a week for five hours a day. But that dedication is not why she was training in the early morning hours. Felix was trying to avoid cameras. She was afraid of losing her sponsorships because she was hiding something. She was 33 years old and about to become a mother.

Professional track & field athletes rely on sponsorships to make a living. They need those contracts to pay for living expenses like any other job, but the fear of losing those deals can be debilitating. In Felix's case, the fear accompanied the excitement of becoming a mother for the first time. Though she was a highly decorated athlete with multiple Olympic and world championship gold medals, and a prominent figure in her sport, she still trained in fear of losing sponsorship.

Many of her sponsors had been good to her over the years. When she turned pro in 2003, one company paid her tuition to finish school and earn a degree in elementary education. She switched to another company in 2010 partly because she felt it was the best place she could empower other women.

Felix recognized her status as a role model in the sport. Other professionals looked up to her, especially young sprinters. She won her first Olympic medal in the 200m at the age of 18. Her success and her fame set her up to be a role model not just in track & field but in sports in general.

So in 2019 she turned her fear into fuel. She decided to join other female athletes who spoke out against sponsors. She wrote an article in the *New York Times*, publicly calling out her shoe sponsor for disagreements in their negotiations. She wanted a guarantee that her pay wouldn't be reduced after her return from maternity leave, but the company would not make this guarantee.

Felix gave birth to her daughter in November 2018, eight weeks early. They remained in the hospital under the constant care of nurses while the premature baby grew in size and strength. At the same time, Felix was in negotiations with her sponsor and strategizing about her return to the track. Although her sponsor did make changes to their maternity policy after Felix and other athletes spoke out, their negotiations together ultimately fell apart.

Felix described pregnancy as the "kiss of death" for female athletes. Could she return to her former status, especially with the Olympics coming up again in 2020? Many had doubts and the global COVID-19 pandemic only made things more difficult for her to return in her mid-30s.

She ran her first race after the baby and COVID in July 2020, focusing on the 400m rather than the 200m. Her time was good enough to earn a spot on the 4x400m Olympic relay team. Unfortunately, the pandemic delayed the Olympics by a year, and she set her sights on a return in 2021.

The following year, Felix made the 400m finals in the Olympics with the lowest qualifying time. She was 10 years older than many of the best runners in the field. She lined up out ahead of all the other athletes in lane 9, generally considered the worst starting lane because you begin in front of all the other athletes. At the start of the race, her pace was a little faster than her usual steady beginning. As the women made the second turn, the other runners in the field seemed poised to pass Felix with ease. As they approached the final 100m, however, she was running side-by-side with two other women in 3rd place. Unfazed, and keeping perfect form, Felix ran through the finish line to win a bronze medal.

With that race she earned her 10th medal, tying Carl Lewis for the highest total of medals by a track & field Olympian in history. She went on to win a gold medal on the 4x400m relay team, passing Carl Lewis for the total medal record (Lewis still held more gold medals). On her feet she wore her own shoe brand, not another sponsor's spikes. In the stands watching Felix's victories was a young girl looking on with pride at her very brave mother.

REFLECTION QUESTIONS

Who looks up to you as a role model on and off the track?

What issues do you feel passionate about the most and why?

What shoe or clothing brands do you like the most and why?

RYAN CROUSER

EXCEL IN ATHLETICS AND ACADEMICS

With his giant 6ft-7in, 300+-pound frame, Ryan Crouser fits the stereotype of a successful shot putter. He often wears his signature cowboy hat over his curly mullet hairstyle, and can be found listening to country music as he trains. Crouser comes from a long line of successful throwers. His grandfather was a noted javelin thrower. His father was an alternate in discus for the Olympics and his uncle was a two-time Olympian in the javelin throw. He has two cousins who have competed at the national level in shot put and discus as well.

As a kid, Crouser wanted to be an astronaut when he grew up. He was a good student and liked school. He played many different sports, but embraced his place as a part of a throwing family. His father worked closely with him during his early teenage years to set him up for success on the national stage.

By the end of his high school career, Crouser broke national records in the shot put and discus. He also took home the gold in the shot put at the World Youth Championship in 2009. At the same championship he earned silver in the discus. The success didn't come without adversity. Crouser struggled with a foot injury in his junior year of high school, and when he moved to the University of Texas to compete for the Longhorns, the struggles with injuries continued.

In addition to his success in track & field, Crouser was also his high school's valedictorian. So while he recovered from foot and hand injuries in his early college years, Crouser made academics his top priority. He studied engineering at first, then switched to economics.

For awhile, it seemed as though school, not sports, promised the most potential for his future. He had won his second national title in the shot put at the 2014 NCAA indoor championship, and he won his third title in the outdoor championships that year. However, he only placed second in the indoor competition and fifth in the outdoor competition in 2015. He had enrolled in a graduate program at Texas to study finance, with the intent of finishing the two-year program in one year.

With one year of eligibility remaining at the NCAA level in 2016, he continued to train in the shot put three days a week after eight hours of classes each day. It was an Olympic year, after all, and he thought he might have a chance to make the team. He began the year by winning the NCAA indoor championship in the shot put again. Then he put almost all of his time and energy into finishing his master's degree in May of that year. The Olympic Trials were just two months after that, so he rapidly increased his training regimen and diet after graduation. Coming into the 2016 trials, Crouser's years of injuries made him relatively unknown compared to the other more successful throwers in the field. The talented Joe Kovacs was the heavy favorite to win the top spot on the USA Olympic team.

Crouser not only beat his fellow American in the 2016 Olympic Trials, he went on to crush Kovacs in the finals, winning the gold medal and setting a new Olympic record in the shot put. After years of uncertainty, injury-free Crouser had finally shown his true potential as an athlete. But now he had a decision to make. Would he follow his love of learning, or his love of sports?

The former high school valedictorian and collegiate honor student decided to combine both loves. He would become a student of the shot put, dedicating both mind and body to becoming the greatest shot putter in the world. He approached his workouts with scientific analysis. He dedicated time and energy into a strict diet of thousands of highly nutritious calories. He experimented with new techniques in the shot-put ring, hoping to continue to improve his form in pursuit of the perfect throw.

It was a brilliant decision. Ryan Crouser went on to win gold again in the 2020 Olympic Games. He has won multiple indoor and outdoor world championships since then, and broken his own Olympic and world records multiple times. In 2021 he was given the Jesse Owens Award by USA Track & Field and named World Male Athlete of the Year by Track & Field News. But he didn't stop there. He continues to compete and win national and world championships.

REFLECTION QUESTIONS

In addition to your athletic goals, what are your academic goals?

How can you study your events and improve your technique?

Are you trying to live up to any family expectations? Does this help or hurt your performance?

KATIE MOON

COMPETE WITH DEDICATION

Before every big pole vault jump, Katie (Nageotte) Moon taps the inside of her spike. On that spike she writes the word "DAD," and has done so for her entire athletic career. When she was 16 years old, her father Mark passed away from a heart attack. Mark, and Katie's mother Diane, had been very supportive of her pole-vaulting dreams at a young age. They took turns driving her an hour away from their home in Olmstead Falls near Cleveland, Ohio to the nearest available practice facility. After Mark died, Moon dedicated her pole-vault career to him.

By her senior year of high school, Moon won state in the pole vault. She had conversations with a number of colleges, but decided to stay in Ohio and compete at the University of Dayton. However she soon felt homesick, and was frustrated with her results in Dayton. So, she transferred to Division II Ashland University near her home in Cleveland. There she won two NCAA Division II championships, and in 2013 earned a psychology degree, with a minor in fashion design. Moon had to decide then if she wanted to trade in her athletic clothing for formal office wear or to try to become a professional track & field athlete.

For Moon to get a sponsorship that could support her as an athlete, she had to do one simple thing: jump at a level that showed she could compete in the Olympics. At first, she continued to work with her college coach. But then she moved to Tennessee to work with an internationally known pole-vaulting coach. Moon found some success, earning enough sponsorship money to fund her preparation for the 2016 Olympics.

She was ranked in the top ten in the country, with a great shot to make the Olympic team. Unfortunately, Moon came in fifth in the trials and didn't make the trip to Rio de Janeiro. It was the first time her training and preparation didn't enable her to reach her goals. Once again, she had to decide whether to keep going and improving or walk away from the sport. She reached out to Brad Walker, a former World Champion pole vaulter who had just retired from competition, and asked him to be her coach.

Coach Walker pushed Moon to work on both the technical and mental approach to pole vaulting. She was working hard, but not pushing herself to the very limits of her ability. Walker taught Moon the meaning and impact of a truly intense work ethic. She responded well. As a result, she moved up from 5th, 6th, and 7th-place finishes to national gold, silver, and bronze medals at various competitions in 2018 and 2019. But in 2020, a global pandemic put Moon's pole vaulting on the backburner again.

Like the rest of the world, Moon went into isolation during 2020. For the first time in her career, she couldn't participate in competitions. Instead, she had to focus on fundamentals, and maintain that highly elite work ethic she learned from her coach. Adversity continued, however, when she contracted COVID in December 2020 during her preparation for the Olympics. She suffered from the brain fog effects of the virus for many months.

Then, a month before the Olympic Trials, Moon traveled home to Ohio for a competition. She discovered that all of her custom-made poles were snapped on the return flight. This was no ordinary setback. Elite pole vaulters have personally-sized poles. Her sponsor said the company couldn't make her new ones in time for the trials. She was forced to look for other options. Thankfully, another company was willing to make new custom-made poles and send them to her within days.

Moon and her family would later laugh that her father Mark had orchestrated some divine intervention. When she used the new poles for the first time, she surprised even herself with the jumps. She set a new personal best, and the best female vault in the world in 2020 with a leap of 4.95m (16ft 2 3/4in) in the Olympic Trials.

Going into the Olympics, she was the favorite to win. She immediately showed the results of her focus on mental toughness. She faulted in her first two jumps and had only one to go. Moon tapped the hand-written "DAD" on the inside of her foot, took 16 steps, and cleared the bar at 4.50m.

Of the 13 women in the competition, only four were able to clear 4.70m, including the reigning world champion, Anzhelika Sidorova. They each cleared 4.85 and moved up to 4.90m, a height which only nine women had ever cleared in history. Everyone missed on the first attempt, then Moon's competitors missed again on their second attempts. Moon lined up once more, tapped her foot, and made her approach. As she stretched her body over the bar, she let out a scream of joy. She landed on the mat as the only person to clear the bar at 4.90m. After another competitor faulted, Moon won gold. With tears of joy she ran into the stands—mostly empty because of the pandemic—to leap into the arms of her coach to thank him.

Katie Moon came home to Cleveland with a gold medal around her neck. Her family and hometown in Northeast Ohio was full of joy. She went on to win gold in the 2022 World Championships. Then during the 2023 World Championships, she tied for best jump in the final. With a giant smile and a hug for her competitor, she chose to share the world title rather than jump again. She had tapped the inside of her spike before each of those winning jumps. She once said in an interview with *Cleveland Magazine*, "Going out and competing in memory of my dad has been all the motivation I've ever needed."

REFLECTION QUESTIONS

If you were to dedicate your competition to one person, who would it be and why?

What are some of your pre-event routines? Where did they come from?

What would happen if you increased the intensity of your work ethic during training?

SYDNEY MCLAUGHLIN-LEVRONE

OVERCOME THE FEAR OF IMPERFECTION

Sydney McLaughlin was destined for greatness. She came from a track family and grew up watching her older siblings compete in meets, with their parents often serving as coaches. The first two McLaughlin kids were good athletes with plenty of accolades. They earned spots on their track teams in college. Sydney, however, was something special.

"Time to unleash the Kraken," her dad thought to himself on the morning of Sydney's first junior meet. She not only won the 300m dash that day, she broke the junior indoor state record. McLaughlin would become a versatile athlete running a wide variety of sprinting events, but her real specialty was the 400m hurdles. She ran a 55.63 as a high school freshman in 2014, just three seconds off the world record. She broke through the 55-second mark in 2016, won the high school national championships, and even earned a spot on the 2016 Olympic team at 17 years old.

That early success instilled in McLaughlin a lot of self-imposed pressure for perfection. She had the ability and she had the experience, now she felt she needed to live up to the hype. The fear of failure was debilitating. She called her father the night before the Olympic Trials begging to go home. When she made the Olympic team, she went to beg her parents to let her quit. But the officials handed her the Team USA uniform and gear before she could even see them. Her father and mother were calm and encouraging. "God has given you a gift...this is the perfect way to get the experience," her father told her.

Months later as she ran in her Olympic semifinal race, she gave into the fear. During the middle of the race she felt her desire to win slip away and slowed down just enough to know she wouldn't make the finals. She decided, "If I can't be perfect, why even try?" Fear of imperfection had defeated her.

She knew her parents were right. It was great to get the experience. She was only 17 years old and had yet to even graduate high school. She came home and finished school, then chose to compete on the track team at the University of Kentucky. When her coach decided to take a job at the University of Texas, McLaughlin decided to turn pro early.

Navigating the life of a professional track athlete was difficult. But with the help of her parents and coaches, she earned some great sponsorship contracts. She moved to Los Angeles and worked with USC hurdles coach Joanna Hayes for a couple of years. Then in 2020 she switched to Hayes's former coach, the legendary Bob Kersee. Despite the lingering fear from 2016, her goal was crystal clear: win an Olympic gold medal and set a world record in the 400m hurdles.

When McLaughlin returned to the Olympic Trials in 2021, something else had changed. She had formed two important relationships. First, she met a young man on Instagram. He was a professional athlete as well, so he understood some of her struggles. But, more importantly to McLaughlin, he was a dedicated Christian man. As their relationship blossomed, so did McLaughlin's relationship with God. She rededicated herself to Jesus Christ, placing her Christian faith at the center of her life. Her relationship with God provided the foundation she needed to break through her fear of failure.

At the trials, she lined up in lane 6. Reigning Olympic champion and world record holder Dalilah Muhammad was right next to her in lane 7. McLaughlin came into the event having lost to Muhammad at the World Athletics Championships two years earlier. Muhammad had set the world record at 52.16s in that race. The Olympic Trial began with Muhammad taking a commanding lead once more. But as Muhammad reached the hurdle to begin the final straight-away, McLaughlin was right at her shoulder. With a final burst of speed and the perfect timing needed to clear the final hurdles, McLaughlin pulled ahead. With a slight lean she crossed the finish line in 51.90 seconds, becoming the first woman to ever run the 400m hurdles in under 52 seconds.

Goal one was complete: world record. Two months later, McLaughlin and Muhammad were set for a rematch at the 2020 Olympic Games in Tokyo. Muhammad took the early lead again. But once again, McLaughlin held a steady pace and then raced to the front with a late sprint. She took the gold medal and broke her own world record with a new time of 51.46s. Goal two was complete.

Back in 2016, McLaughlin had let her fear of imperfection hold her back. In 2021 she achieved that perfection in the hurdles, ironically, by letting go of the desire to be perfect in the first place. She was free from the fear. Free to focus on what mattered most to her. Later, in her autobiography, she would write, "Fear is a product of misplaced priorities. It comes from valuing the wrong thing too much. But when you value Jesus above all else, he takes your fear and replaces it with faith" (*Far Beyond Gold*, page 204).

Two weeks after winning the gold medal, she announced her engagement to Andre Levrone, the man of faith she met on Instagram. In May of 2022 they were married and only a month later Sydney McLaughlin-Levrone crushed her own world record. Now she was not only the first woman to run under 52 seconds, she became the first to run under 51 seconds with a time of 50.68. She is fearless.

REFLECTION QUESTIONS

What are some of the fears holding you back from success?

Do you have any misplaced priorities?

Does faith help you overcome fear? If not, what has helped you the most to ignore fears of failure?

TRACK & FIELD EVENTS

SPRINTS

100m

200m

400m

HURDLES

110m hurdles

400m hurdles

DISTANCE

800m

1500m (or 1600m, mile run)

3000m (or 3200m, two-mile run)

5000m

10,000m

Marathon

RELAYS

4x100m relay

4x400m relay

JUMPS

Long Jump

Triple Jump

High Jump

Pole Vault

THROWS

Shot Put

Discus

Javelin Throw

Hammer Throw

COMBINED EVENTS

Pentathlon

Heptathlon

Decathlon

ABOUT THE AUTHOR

JARED DEES is an education creator, speaker, and author of twenty books. He is best known as the creator of The Religion Teacher (TheReligionTeacher.com), a popular website that provides practical resources and teaching strategies for religious educators. He holds master's degrees in education and theology from the University of Notre Dame. He frequently gives keynotes and leads workshops at conferences, church events, and school in-services throughout the year on a variety of topics. He lives near South Bend, Indiana, with his wife and children.

Jared developed a love for track & field at a young age. He was the captain of his high school track team and went on to coach at both the high school and middle school levels for many years.

Learn more about Jared's books, speaking events, and other projects at jareddees.com.

ALSO BY JARED DEES

31 Days to Becoming a Better Religious Educator

To Heal, Proclaim, and Teach

Christ in the Classroom

Beatitales

Tales of the Ten Commandments

Do Not Be Afraid

Take and Eat

Pray without Ceasing

Take Up Your Cross

Prepare the Way

Advent with the Angels

15-Minute Stations of the Cross for Kids

The Angelus & Regina Caeli

Just Plant Seeds

The Gospel According to Video Games

Made in the USA
Middletown, DE
28 July 2024